BIRTHDAY BOOK
Donated to Yalesville Elementary School
Library Media Center
In honor of
Amy Thai's 8th birthday
September 17, 2006

The Sunset Switch

by KATHLEEN V. KUDLINSKI

illustrated by LINDY BURNETT

NORTHWORD PRESS

Minnetonka, Minnesota

Note to Readers:
Look at each animal page carefully and you'll discover hidden surprises! The homes of the opposite daytime or nighttime animal can be seen in each picture.

The illustrations were created using gouache
The text and display type were set in Papyrus and Indy Italic
Composed in the United States of America
Designed by Lois A. Rainwater
Edited by Kristen McCurry

Text © 2005 by Kathleen V. Kudlinski
Illustrations © 2005 by Lindy Burnett

NORTHWORD
Books for Young Readers

11571 K-Tel Drive
Minnetonka, MN 55343
www.tnkidsbooks.com

Library of Congress Cataloging-in-Publication Data

Kudlinski, Kathleen V.
The sunset switch / by Kathleen V. Kudlinski ; illustrated by Lindy Burnett.
p. cm.
ISBN 1-55971-916-8
1. Animals--Juvenile literature. 2. Nocturnal animals--Juvenile literature. I. Burnett, Lindy, ill. II. Title.

QL49.K89 2005

591.5'18--dc22   2004024139

Printed in Singapore
10 9 8 7 6 5 4 3 2 1

Slowly the sun slips from the sky.
Day animals grow sleepy.
Night animals start to stir and wake.
Come and watch them trade places.
The sunset switch is beginning.

Settle down, sleepy Swallow.
Sunset has come.

You raced mosquitoes through the sky all day.
Tuck your head beneath your wing, close your eyes, and sleep.

Open your eyes, little Bat.
The sun is gone.

It's your turn to chase mosquitoes.
Unwrap your wings, yawn, and stretch. Wake up, little Bat.

Good night, Goshawk.
Your daytime turn is over.

You searched the meadows for mice all day.
Fluff your fine feathers, and sleep.

Rise and shine, Screech Owl.
The moon is drifting up in the tree.

Flap your silent wings and go about your mouse search.

Sweet dreams,
groggy Gray Squirrel.

You hunted nuts and seeds all day,
scampering through the treetops.
Cuddle up with your tail now, and sleep.

Wake up, Flying Squirrel,
tucked in your secret space. Night has come.

It's your turn to go gliding through the trees, hunting seeds and nuts. Jump out of bed, Flying Squirrel.

Shut your droopy eyes,
Snowy Egret.

You had your turn all day,
stalking the swamp for fish and frogs.
Stomach full now, you should snooze.

Heads up, Night Heron.
It's your breakfast time.

The swamp has more tasty swimmers ready for stalking.
Shake a leg, hungry Heron.

Nighty-night, weary Butterfly.

You sipped sweet nectar all day.
Tongue coiled, wings folded, you should be sleeping.

Up and at 'em, lazy Moth!
Can't you smell the flowers?

Flutter to their scents and sip nectar through the night.
Get moving, Moth.

Snuggle in,
Smooth Green Snake.

All day long, you slithered and snapped after beetles and bugs. Curl up cozy now, under your rock.

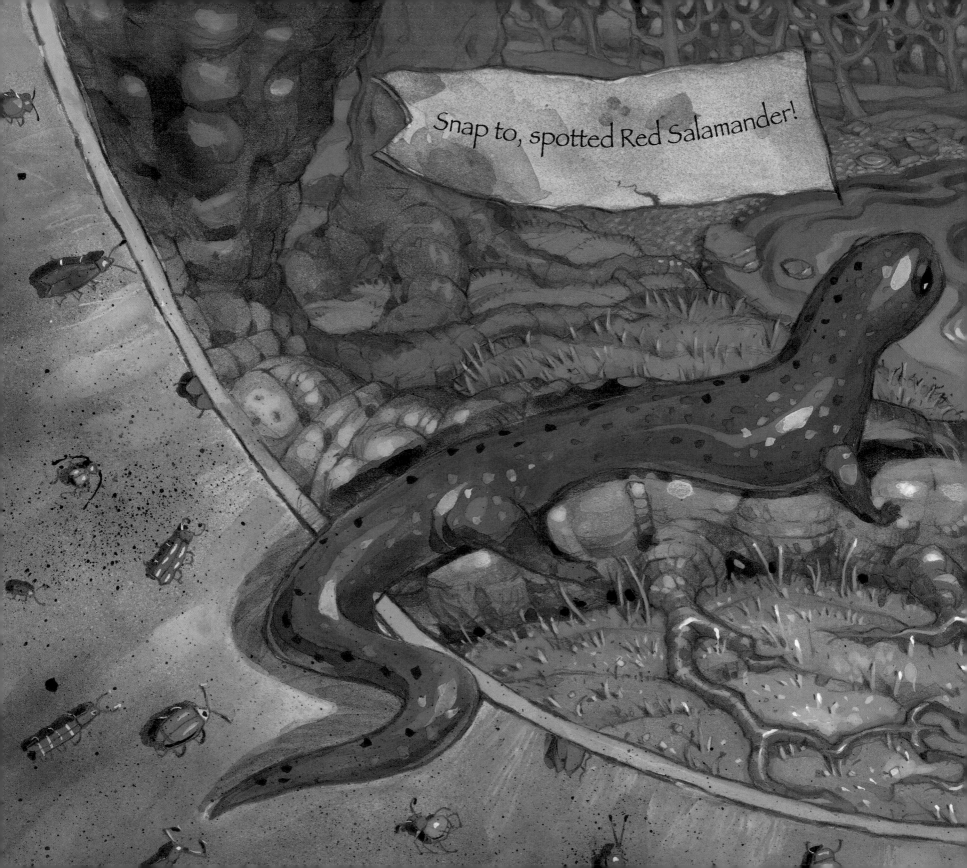

It's time to creep and crawl, and catch your insect meals.
Hurry now, lazybones, or you'll miss your turn!

Slowly the sun creeps back into the sky.

Night animals are sleepy.

Day animals start to stir and wake.

It is time to trade places again.

The sunrise switch is about to begin.

KATHLEEN KUDLINSKI's first love was nature. She taught science in elementary schools for seven years and she is now the author of twenty-seven books and a prize-winning newspaper columnist. A Master Teaching Artist for the State of Connecticut, she visits classrooms as often as possible. Ms. Kudlinski lives beside a deep, wild lake in Guilford, Connecticut.

LINDY BURNETT is an award-winning advertising illustrator, but she says the real fun began when she started illustrating children's books. *The Sunset Switch* is her fourth book for children. Many of the critters in this book can be found near Ms. Burnett's home in Madison, Georgia, where she lives with her three Jack Russell terriers.